Ᏽ ᎥᎠᏛᏋᏍ

ᏬᏗᏖᏳᏋᏋᏏ ᏒᏍᎧ ᏱᎠᏳᏬᏮᏖ

ᏱᏳᏖᏖ Ꮛ Ᏻ Ꮼᏽ

ᏍᏬᏽᏍᎧ ᏋᏍᎧᏖ

 NCE UPON A TIME in the islands called the Philippines, where sea stars bloom in a shimmering emerald sea, there lived a fisherman named Abak, his wife Abadesa, and their beautiful daughter Abadeha. Underneath a happy sun and graceful coconut palms, the house where they lived was a castle of joy to little Abadeha.

When Abadeha was thirteen, her mother suddenly became ill and died. She was buried in the cool shade of a nearby forest, leaving behind a daughter and a husband whose hearts were filled with sorrow and tears. Abadeha felt that her carefree world had suddenly crumbled.

Sometime later, on a trip to another island, Abak met a widow with two daughters. The lonely widower married the woman and brought the stepfamily home, hoping that they would make a loving family for him and Abadeha.

THE STEPMOTHER IMMEDIATELY saw how plain and mean-spirited her daughters were compared to Abadeha's beauty and kindness. She secretly swore to make her new stepdaughter's life miserable. Of course, Abak had no knowledge of his new wife's evil side.

With a large family to support, Abak had to go on more fishing trips that took him away for long periods of time. In his absence, Stepmother began treating Abadeha harshly. She made Abadeha work from morning to night, cleaning the house, fetching water from the river, cooking all the meals, and tending the stove.

"Why do you love to powder your face with soot, Kitchen Princess?" The stepsisters would mock her. Their constant taunting was now a part of Abadeha's life. Tired, sooty, and sweaty, she would fall asleep each night on the kitchen floor.

WHENEVER ABADEHA WAS tired and tried to rest, Stepmother would grab a broom and swing it through the air to harass her. "You good-for-nothing, lazy girl, next time I will whip you with the tail of a stingray!" Stepmother would screech at the top of her voice.

One morning, while Abadeha was scouring clay pots in the kitchen, Stepmother threw two handkerchiefs in Abadeha's face and ordered, "Wash these two handkerchiefs until the white one turns black and the black one turns white. Do exactly as I tell you, or I will whip you until your bones crack."

Sadly, Abadeha went to the river bank. Sitting beneath the shade of a leafy bamboo, she watched the clear water freely flowing downstream. She remembered the life she had before her mother passed away, frcc and happy.

ALONE SHE WEPT. Through her tears, she cried out,

> "Mother, Oh, Mother,
> Bathala, Creator of the Earth,
> Anitos, Spirits of my ancestors,
> Hear me and help me, please."

At the water's edge, the wind softly rustled the leaves of the trees. Abadeha turned and saw a beautiful woman bathed in radiant light. Her gentle face was full of kindness. "I am the Spirit of the Forest, the faithful guardian of all that live and grow here. I have come because I have heard your cry for help. Do not worry. Your patience and hard work will be rewarded one day."

Gently, she took the two handkerchiefs from Abadeha's hand and waved them with a flick in the air.

OUT OF NOWHERE two more spirits appeared, a man and a woman. They bowed to Abadeha and each took a handkerchief. Together they began a magical dance. Spinning about with delicate steps, they playfully chased each other. Pulling and tossing the handkerchiefs, they gracefully waved their arms above their heads. Round and round, faster and faster, swift as a whirlpool they went! Then suddenly they stopped, and handed the handkerchiefs back to Abadeha. Amazingly, the white handkerchief was now black, and the black one was white.

Abadeha hurried home to give the handkerchiefs to Stepmother.

"So, our Kitchen Princess was able to do this," snorted Stepmother.

For the first time, Stepmother had lost a chance to make Abadeha suffer.

THE NEXT MORNING Stepmother was still furious about the night before, and she continued to make demands on Abadeha. Abadeha had to spread newly harvested rice on a mat to dry in the sun, then she was to pound, winnow, and cook the rice for the evening meal.

While Abadeha was busy in the kitchen, a hungry pig wandered into the yard and gobbled up the drying rice, tearing the mat into tatters and shreds with its sharp hooves. Stepmother watched the whole time and did nothing until the pig left. Then triumphantly, she called in Abadeha, and screamed into her ear, as she pulled on her hair, "Careless girl, see what the pig did to the rice and the mat! You must weave the ruined mat back into one whole piece again!"

CARRYING THE TATTERED MAT, Abadeha cried all the way to the river bank where the Spirit of the Forest had appeared before.

"Mother, Oh, Mother,
Bathala, Creator of the Earth,
Anitos, Spirits of my ancestors,
Hear me and help me, please."

This time the Spirit of the Forest quickly appeared, and clapped her hands three times. In the wink of an eye, a group of young female spirits surfaced and started to weave the mat skillfully back together. In just a few moments the mat was entirely new again.

Before Abadeha could thank them, the Spirit of the Forest took out a sarimanok, a chicken with a long flowing tail and feathers the color of the rainbow. "Take this with you. It is now yours."

Abadeha said in awe, "I have never seen a more beautiful bird. I am so grateful for your kindness."

Carefully, she put the sarimanok and the mat under her arms and started the walk home.

STEPMOTHER WAS QUITE ANNOYED when she saw the fully restored mat. "If I ever find out how you are cheating me, you will be in terrible trouble. And where did you get that wild bird?" Stepmother said while grabbing the sarimanok from Abadeha's arm.

"But, it is my pet," Abadeha pleaded.

"I will take care of this bird for you," Stepmother replied with a twisted smile.

Early the next morning while Abadeha was sweeping the yard, Stepmother took the sarimanok from the coop, and without any warning, chopped its head and feet off with a knife. She went straight to the kitchen and began roasting the bird. As Abadeha came to the kitchen and saw the lifeless feet of the sarimanok, she began crying bitter tears.

Stepmother said maliciously, "This bird is big and fat. Dinner tonight will be delicious."

Weeping, Abadeha gathered the sarimanok's feet and ran to the river.

WHEN ABADEHA REACHED THE RIVER, the Spirit of the Forest was there to meet her.

"If my stepmother could do this to my pet, she could do the same to me." Abadeha sobbed as she realized the danger around her.

Tenderly, the Spirit spoke, "Do not be afraid, my child. Go bury the sarimanok's feet by your mother's grave and pray to your ancestors."

Obediently, Abadeha did what she was told, and she planted a little garden around her mother's grave. Then she knelt down and prayed, "Since you left, oh, dear mother, the days are longer, the work is harder. My tears are flowing like a river. If I could touch you in my heart, I would be stronger."

As if heaven was answering her prayer, a warm, gentle rain began to fall and wash away her tears.

THE RAINY SEASON CAME and left before Abadeha went back to her mother's grave. Miraculously, where she had planted the sarimanok's feet, there had grown an enchanted tree laden with treasures. Rings, bracelets, necklaces, earrings, pearls, diamonds, and golden gowns all hung from the boughs. Abadeha was excited to have found this unusual tree, yet she decided to keep it a secret, and only took a few pieces of jewelry with her.

Returning home, Abadeha hid the pieces in an old trunk in the granary. When she went into the house, Stepmother was already waiting for her.

"Where have you been? You are trying to get away from work again," the cruel woman said harshly as she threw a blanket at Abadeha. "Now, mend the blanket this instant."

Poor Abadeha slowly picked up the blanket and went to the corner of the kitchen. There, even though piles of work awaited her, she found solace by the warm stove.

WHILE HUNTING IN THE FOREST one day, the handsome son of the island chieftain saw a sarimanok. He followed it to Abadeha's secret garden. The prince could not believe his eyes when he caught sight of the tree. He immediately understood that it must be a magical tree. He took out tobacco leaves and betel nuts from his bag and respectfully laid them in front of the trunk. Then he knelt down and bowed his head.

"Bathala, and Spirit of the Forest, forgive me for stepping on your sacred ground. Please accept my humble offerings and allow me to receive one of your precious gifts from the tree." The prince picked a ring from a branch and slipped it onto his finger.

That evening at home, the prince's finger began to swell. He called out to Datu, his father.

"Father, my finger hurts badly, and I can not remove this ring," the prince said with a shaking voice, his face distorted with pain.

DATU SENT FOR THE **B**ABAYLAN, the priest-healer, right away. The Babaylan performed a ritual but failed to remove the ring. He could help very little except to say, "Listen to your heart. It will tell you what to do."

The night wore on and the pain in the prince's finger became unbearable. In a fevered dream, a sarimanok came to him with an orchid in its beak. The prince took the flower and kissed it. All of a sudden the flower turned into a beautiful maiden. She opened her hand and showed him a ring. The prince looked down at his hand and the ring was no longer on his finger.

The prince woke up in a heavy sweat and told his father what was revealed to him in the dream. Datu quickly summoned the island messenger and ordered, "Beat your drums! Tell everyone that the girl who can remove the ring from my son's finger will be his bride."

THE MESSENGER WASTED NO TIME. By midday he had spread the news to all the islands. A great number of unmarried girls flocked to see the prince, but none of them could remove the ring.

When Abadeha heard about the ring, she asked for permission to go.

"You do not deserve to see the prince. Your place is in the kitchen." Stepmother pushed Abadeha inside and locked the door.

As Stepmother lay down on a hammock for her nap, the Spirit of the Forest appeared and unlocked the door. "The prince is waiting for you," she told Abadeha with a smile. "Go now and see him."

ABADEHA'S STEPSISTERS were at the prince's royal house when she arrived.

"How dare you come here!" the first one snarled.

"Look at yourself. You are so filthy!" the second one said with a glare.

The prince heard the commotion and signaled, "Let her come near."

Everyone looked on in disbelief as Abadeha in her ragged clothes approached the prince. Lovingly she took the prince's hand and gently removed the ring from his finger. The prince was overjoyed and kissed Abadeha's hands. He exclaimed as he pressed her hands against his heart, "You are the one! Today you shall be my bride."

ALL THE PEOPLE ON THE ISLANDS of the Philippines rejoiced at the wedding of Abadeha and the prince. Dancers, singers, musicians, poets, and magicians put on their best performances to celebrate the largest and the merriest wedding anyone had ever seen. Abadeha wore the golden gown and the jewelry from the enchanted tree to her wedding. Hovering happily nearby was the Spirit of the Forest, Abadeha's very special guest whom only she could see.

Abadeha's father came home just in time for the occasion. He was sad that Abadeha had to endure such suffering while he was away, but he was proud of her courage. As for Stepmother and her two daughters, the prince banished them to the chicken yard where they spent the rest of their lives.

Abadeha and her prince shared their happiness and wealth with the people on the islands. They enjoyed a long life of harmony, peace, and love.

AUTHOR'S NOTE

Abadeha: the Philippine Cinderella is a reconstruction of the Cinderella story from traditional Philippine folklore. Like many other Filipino folk tales, this story has disappeared from mainstream Philippine folk literature—a casualty of more than three hundred years of Spanish colonization and a century of Americanization. Recognizing the critical need for the preservation of pre-colonial Philippine culture and arts, I saw significant possibilities in reviving this beautiful tale from its rich and indigenous roots.

The obedient Abadeha mirrors the general concept of how a child should act in Philippine society. The stepmother's threat to whip Abadeha with the tail of a stingray is consistent with the character of the "evil mother" and the hyperbolic nature of fairy tales. In reality, a similar threat from a Filipino parent is never carried out and is simply a way to drive fear into the heart of a willful child. In the home, the whip is a symbol of discipline of last resort, which generally parents never find a reason to use.

Using the native names of the characters as scaffolding, I pulled together local religious beliefs and practices in retelling the story, and incorporated native flora, fauna, and linguistic terms. The title page of the book is done in *Alibata*—the ancient and now forgotten system of writing. This story deals with the universal issues of sibling rivalry and mother-stepdaughter conflicts, and conveys the importance and rewards of hard work, kindness, patience, perseverance, faith, hope, and love—everything a young girl is supposed to learn in her journey on the enchanted and sometimes torturous path towards womanhood.

Text copyright ©2001 by Myrna J. de la Paz
Illustration copyright ©2001 by Youshan Tang
Book Design by Menagerie Design
Printed in Hong Kong
Published by Shen's Books
8625 Hubbard Road
Auburn, CA 95602-7815
www.shens.com
800-456-6660

Library of Congress Cataloging-in-Publication Data
De La Paz, Myrna J.
Abadeha : the Philippine Cinderella /
written by Myrna J. de la Paz ; illustrated by Youshan Tang.
p. cm.
Summary: In this version of Cinderella, set in the Philippines,
Abadeha endures abuse by her stepmother before being helped by the Spirit of the Forest
and becoming the bride of the island chieftain's son.
ISBN 1-885008-17-1
[1. Fairy tales, 2. Folklore—Philippines.] I. Tang, Youshan, ill. II. Title.
PZ8 .D372 2001 398.2—dc21   00-066074